# Children of the Reverie

## Hour II

By Briana Jade Dobson

*To the people who stood by my side in my trials.*

# Table of Contents

# Introduction

**Therefore**, brethren, stand fast, and hold the traditions which ye have been taught, whether by word, or our epistle," ( 2 Thessalonians 2:15). Throughout history, in every story, each hero has a quest and that quest begins with a want for better or just the hero being completely lost after something shaking has occurred. In the essence of it all, they find themselves. They find this greater, stronger person they never knew they were and when that happens they are faced with a new villain, worse than their first adversary, but the journey has molded and formed them to be strong enough to defeat this villain. If you think of your life, your wins and loses. They're not really loses, they are just trainings. When you win, you only smile when you have defeated the villain.

God must send us all on that very same journey that David had to go on. From zealous, to broken, to king. If you are going to rule someday, then God knows you have to be trained mentally, spiritually, and emotionally. You have to be controlled, not easily shaken by a tiny change in the tides. If a tide goes one way, your ship goes that way too, even if it means destruction. No. God doesn't want you to be a ruler like that. And if taking you through this cave, dragging you around this bend, forcing you to stare your fears in the face, then He will do it.

Along this quest, though He will be there and at times He might pretend to leave you just to see if you will be faithful. You will want to break. Want to split and do all the above but keep going because of your frustration, but there is always God still there reminding you of those who came before, who are still cheering for you when Satan is in your ear telling you to end it here and now, knowing that if he can get you to do that, you will be one less person he has to worry about. Through your tears, crying, and screaming, knowing that you could end it all here and now is anything in this world really worth that much, when it shall all pass away in a blink of an eye? Should you compromise your destiny for something that won't even have value in another few years? All good things must come to an end and that is a guarantee because God knows if you become too comfortable in this life you wouldn't care about the afterlife with Him. You wouldn't care to always keep moving and you would become sanitary and dirty like ponds and God doesn't need a pond for his spirit to dwell in but a forever moving river. By the end of this life, you will be a river, flowing like the Amazon River with life and giving life.

# Living in Twilight

# Mirage Du Crépuscule

---

A figure of clear air racing into the forest only to appear and vanish in before my eyes.

Mirage du crépuscule, where hath thou gone to where I cannot find you?

And how can this be, when you were me and I were you and yet I lost you again?

A hand that fadeth right through mine, when I reach for your hand.

Mirage du crépuscule, where hath thou gone to where I cannot find you?

And how can this be, when you were me and I were you and yet I lost you again?

A shadow stabbing me through my heart and I die before your eyes for you have returned but you were too late.

Mirage du crépuscule, where hath thou gone to where I cannot find you?

And how can this be, when you were me and I were you and yet I lost you again?

A time when we both were just the atmosphere, not even a part of this capsule of sadness.

Mirage du crépuscule, where hath thou gone to where I cannot find you?

And how can this be, when you were me and I were you and yet I lost you again?

A long time ago your spirit and mine were kin, but here we are pin without memory of another.

Mirage du crépuscule, where hath thou gone to where I cannot find you?

And how can this be, when you were me and I were you and yet I lost you again?

A look into a mirror, a flash of what we used to be whenever we touch it but cannot feel the touch of another's hand.

Mirage du crépuscule, where hath thou gone to where I cannot find you?

And how can this be, when you were me and I were you and yet I lost you again?

A look into your eyes, a look into mine and we know, but we don't know what we know.

Mirage du crépuscule, where hath thou gone to where I cannot find you?

And how can this be, when you were me and I were you and yet I lost you again?

A mind that cracks into insanity, a heart that breaks like the strings of the harp that David once held.

Mirage du crépuscule, where hath thou gone to where I cannot find you?

And how can this be, when you were me and I were you and yet I lost you again?

A fear that is so great we're blinded, a turbulence so strong we're pulled apart.

Mirage du crépuscule, where hath thou gone to where I cannot find you?

And how can this be, when you were me and I were you and yet I lost you again?

A glimpse of your cloak and I know who you are, but I do not know if you are the dark rider that stabbed my heart long ago.

Mirage du crépuscule, where hath thou gone to where I cannot find you?

And how can this be, when you were me and I were you and yet I lost you again?

A lake that stares back, but cannot speak for it has no mouth so it rushes against the stones to roar with fury of the ones who fell victim to his anger.

Mirage du crépuscule, where hath thou gone to where I cannot find you?

And how can this be, when you were me and I were you and yet I lost you again?

A voice that whispers into our ears and tells us, but we're convinced it is only a trap of sin.

Mirage du crépuscule, where hath thou gone to where I cannot find you?

And how can this be, when you were me and I were you and yet I lost you again?

A lie that sprouts from their mouths and into a fire that seeks to burn us alive.

Mirage du crépuscule, where hath thou gone to where I cannot find you?

And how can this be, when you were me and I were you and yet I lost you again?

A breath that hurts to take for my heart is overtaken by the arrows that stung it.

Mirage du crépuscule, where hath thou gone to where I cannot find you?

And how can this be, when you were me and I were you and yet I lost you again?

A pain that can be quenched to make me smile even in death when you were here.

Mirage du crépuscule, where hath thou gone to where I cannot find you?

And how can this be, when you were me and I were you and yet I lost you again?

A lifetime compared to days is no match, although it is yet just a half glass.

Mirage du crépuscule, where hath thou gone to where I cannot find you?

And how can this be, when you were me and I were you and yet I lost you again?

A grin on loneliness's face when he is moved by the prison I have been thrown away to without a cause.

Mirage du crépuscule, where hath thou gone to where I cannot find you?

And how can this be, when you were me and I were you and yet I lost you again?

A tree in a desert that turns out to be more sand and just a glimpse of what this heart ached for most.

Mirage du crépuscule, where hath thou gone to where I cannot find you?

And how can this be, when you were me and I were you and yet I lost you again?

A figure that taps me on the shoulder, but when I turn I only see that shattered glass.

Mirage du crépuscule, where hath thou gone to where I cannot find you?

And how can this be, when you were me and I were you and yet I lost you again?

# In Another Lifetime

---

There was a crown of royalty bestowed upon my head.

In another world; in another lifetime I knew this person I now call a stranger.

A golden ring of happiness was placed in my hand.

In another world; in another lifetime I knew this person I now call a stranger.

The world was whole and there was no need for tears for there was music.

In another world; in another lifetime I knew this person I now call a stranger.

Your eyes sparkled with the innocence of a child, which sometimes shows but quickly fades now.

In another world; in another lifetime I knew this person I now call a stranger.

The rivers were plentiful and settled so we were able to race through them on long afternoons.

In another world; in another lifetime I knew this person I now call a stranger.

My heart felt as if it were filled with butterflies when you were near.

In another world; in another lifetime I knew this person I now call a stranger.

I had no need for riches for I had my heaven inside my heart with you.

In another world; in another lifetime I knew this person I now call a stranger.

The world was joyous in dance and psaltery and harp beneath the stars and moon.

In another world; in another lifetime I knew this person I now call a stranger.

It was those nights that I remembered what it meant to have a sun and a moon, neither could work without another and neither could we.

In another world; in another lifetime I knew this person I now call a stranger.

# True Love

---

Doesn't boast or is sure to make it known to everyone.
For the actions and hearts of a pair are enough.
True love.
Doesn't feel as if it needs to fight to keep it in check.
For if one loves another they are too significant in their life for them to think of others.
True love.
Doesn't tire or die like other things in this life that are fragile.
For it is that gift that God has given us that is dependable.
True love.
Doesn't go one way or make one feel lesser than a human.
For if one is glorified then love helps it shine brighter.
True love.
Doesn't break in halves or is for a moment then on with the next.

For it can only be magnified if it is teal and becomes more radiant.

True love.

Doesn't fail to heal or fail to satisfy a starving heart of emptiness.

For it can reach those inner hunger that nothing else can.

True love.

Doesn't allow you to kill or harm your other half but protect that part of your heart.

For if the other half is harmed then the heart faileth to function.

True love.

Doesn't allow tears to be shed or bears to tear.

For tears are a sign that somehow a part is failing.

True love.

Doesn't play with pride or allow it to enter the door.

For if pride is present love cannot sit in a house of enmity and hate.

True love.

Doesn't feel the need to step on the other to prove its power.

For if power is in need to be in place, then what happens to balance.

True love.

Doesn't have a need for two perfectionists or perfection at all just the best game we have.

For if we were perfectionists, then where were the growth and development of love to be strengthened.

True love.

Doesn't have to be about what you can buy with money or how much time you are away to gain things.

For if we were brought by things, we would have no need for knights that earned love by pureness of hearts to fight dragons in order to wake us from the slumber of death.

True love.

Doesn't feel trodden afoot when life collapses or runs away like a fleeing horse in the eye of a storm.

For if love were fear, there'd be no place for happiness to flourish and blossom.

True love.

# The Very Thing

---

Ash burned corpses of what used to be.

All I do is watch. All I can do is stand helplessly above my beloved city.

Because the very thing I long for is the very thing I cannot have and the very thing I do not seek is right at my fingertips.

Bones remains of the ship that those sailors sought to sail a time ago.

All I do is watch. All I can do is stand helplessly above my beloved city.

Because the very thing I long for is the very thing I cannot have and the very thing I do not seek is right at my fingertips.

Slippers, sitting sadly on a shelf of a dream that was lost.

All I do is watch. All I can do is stand helplessly above my beloved city.

Because the very thing I long for is the very thing I cannot have and the very thing I do not seek is right at my fingertips.

Ghost, friends of my fears that haunt my very soul and vex me.

All I do is watch. All I can do is stand helplessly above my beloved city.

Because the very thing I long for is the very thing I cannot have and the very thing I do not seek is right at my fingertips.

Speech, impaired to the ears that have been placed on my heels.

All I do is watch. All I can do is stand helplessly above my beloved city.

Because the very thing I long for is the very thing I cannot have and the very thing I do not seek is right at my fingertips.

Evil, the most realistic waltz of these most modern and humane times.

All I do is watch. All I can do is stand helplessly above my beloved city.

Because the very thing I long for is the very thing I cannot have and the very thing I do not seek is right at my fingertips.

Focus, set ablaze in the campfire along with the other notes burned that night.

All I do is watch. All I can do is stand helplessly above my beloved city.

Because the very thing I long for is the very thing I cannot have and the very thing I do not seek is right at my fingertips.

# Home Absent

---

Not a place, not even a building but a feeling in our hearts of warmth and happiness.

But what happens when you get there to the place you once found it and now it is absent?

It shines in the midst when everything goes wrong, it stands tall for you to come back to and take protection.

But what happens when you get there to the place you once found it and now it is absent?

If the view melts away in the tremendous fire that gnaws it away my heart will scream for everything it lost there.

But what happens when you get there to the place you once found it and now it is absent?

There is no need for a sun, nor a moon for guidance for when home is present I know exactly what I'm looking for in my heart.

But what happens when you get there to the place you once found it and now it is absent?

Tears have no need in the sight of home for he smiles upon me so that I cannot cry.

But what happens when you get there to the place you once found it and now it is absent?

Words from those evil can only plop from off my heels when I'm in the tracks to home.

But what happens when you get there to the place you once found it and now it is absent?

A place I can look to and know that it knows exactly what I feel without a word or motion.

But what happens when you get there to the place you once found it and now it is absent?

Simple is it, but as magnificent as having millions of mansions, and for once my heart is satisfied beyond comparison.

But what happens when you get there to the place you once found it and now it is absent?

Money and work are always at hand and you'll always need or want more of it, but a home is fulfilling to the fullest as if it is the thing the soul longed for most.

But what happens when you get there to the place you once found it and now it is absent?

# If We Both Remember

---

The time of happiness, where the world was still.

If we both remember, then perhaps our hearts can fly once again.

The laughter of the past will never cease to exist.

If we both remember, then perhaps our hearts can fly once again.

The passage back to when we were together could open.

If we both remember, then perhaps our hearts can fly once again.

The light won't fade but expand past the bridges of darkness.

If we both remember, then perhaps our hearts can fly once again.

It can all come back alive with our hearts united at last.

If we both remember, then perhaps our hearts can fly once again.

The tears in which we had forgotten why we shed will have been for a reason.

If we both remember, then perhaps our hearts can fly once again.

The mind will have forgotten, but if the hearts collide the light of memory will shine.

If we both remember, then perhaps our hearts can fly once again.

The hope in which we bear upon our shoulders will no longer burden us.

If we both remember, then perhaps our hearts can fly once again.

The truth which had been foretold will have come true, so the evil will see.

If we both remember, then perhaps our hearts can fly once again.

# Once Upon a Time that Never Existed

---

I wasn't this person with a hand to hold and a person to walk side by side.

Once upon a time that never existed.

I didn't die by the wayside of the river but was saved at the last moment.

Once upon a time that never existed.

I didn't have this fear, this fear that things wouldn't turn out alright.

Once upon a time that never existed.

I didn't have to fear that I would dance or waltz alone in this ballroom inside my memory with ghosts and phantoms.

Once upon a time that never existed.

I wasn't this person confused and in turmoil inside and outside.

Once upon a time that never existed.

I wasn't this person just wading by the rivers of Jordan for something impossible in a dark world.

Once upon a time that never existed.

I didn't have to constantly question whether or not I would find someone while watching others run off into happily ever and me trapped in this happily never after every time.

Once upon a time that never existed.

I'm not important enough to just disappear and I'm not unimportant enough to be here.

Once upon a time that never existed.

I was with this masked person dancing all night beneath the starry skies, that went on endlessly.

Once upon a time that never existed.

I was awakened like sleeping beauty and found that I was once dead and brought to life.

Once upon a time that never existed.

I wasn't this forsaken rose without a thorny crown to belong to.

Once upon a time that never existed.

I wasn't this person that dreaded everything about this world.

Once upon a time that never existed.

I wasn't this person pinned between doom if you do and doomed if you don't.

Once upon a time that never existed.

I was able to ride away from the castle and forget about the evil dragon.

Once upon a time that never existed.

# And Even If We Did

---

See all the same people except for one. Go to the same places without the one.

And even if we did go back to the past places it wouldn't be the same.

Because without that one happiness is absent and so is that spirit.

Make all the same friends, play all the same games without that one.

And even if we did go back to the past places it wouldn't be the same.

Because without that one happiness is absent and so is that spirit.

Draw the same ways, run the same pace without the one, it's all for nothing.

And even if we did go back to the past places it wouldn't be the same.

Because without that one happiness is absent and so is that spirit.

Use the same techniques the one trained, do it the exact same way it'll always miss.

And even if we did go back to the past places it wouldn't be the same.

Because without that one happiness is absent and so is that spirit.

Dive deep into the blue, swim halfway across the sea looking lost without the one, who will forever be waving to you below the deep blue.

And even if we did go back to the past places it wouldn't be the same.

Because without that one happiness is absent and so is that spirit.

Race for the light, fly to the skies without the one wing we'll be torn to shreds.

And even if we did go back to the past places it wouldn't be the same.

Because without that one happiness is absent and so is that spirit.

Go for the same goals, test the tested without the one it means a bag of worms.

And even if we did go back to the past places it wouldn’t be the same.

Because without that one happiness is absent and so is that spirit.

Translated from one world to the other, teleported to three worlds without the one I can’t tell one from the other.

And even if we did go back to the past places it wouldn’t be the same.

Because without that one happiness is absent and so is that spirit.

# One Indeed

---

Thy name shall be mine and in time thy name becomes a lesser fine that is paid.

And if God makes us one, we shall be one indeed going twice as more than before.

When one and one come together two is made and at heart is the lamb, our crown and glory.

Forbidden is your secret as is mine, but the secret is not hidden from our hearts.

And if God makes us one, we shall be one indeed.

When one and one come together two is made and at heart is the lamb, our crown and glory.

A cloak of gold shall hover above our heads like a halo to cover us from the world.

And if God makes us one, we shall be one indeed.

When one and one come together two is made and at heart is the lamb, our crown and glory.

Thy hand shall be as lock and my hand shall be thy key that only you receive.

And if God makes us one, we shall be one indeed.

When one and one come together two is made and at heart is the lamb, our crown and glory.

There shall be no mountain too tall, no river too long that can stop me from reaching to you and you to me.

And if God makes us one, we shall be one indeed.

When one and one come together two is made and at heart is the lamb, our crown and glory.

Man can tell, man can sell, but man cannot bell when the time is right.

And if God makes us one, we shall be one indeed.

When one and one come together two is made and at heart is the lamb, our crown and glory.

Running bringing song and stringed instruments like fairies from fairy tales.

And if God makes us one, we shall be one indeed.

When one and one come together two is made and at heart is the lamb, our crown and glory.

Jewels can't be compared to the preciousness of the day God has placed for us to be joined.

And if God makes us one, we shall be one indeed.

When one and one come together two is made and at heart is the lamb, our crown and glory.

Crowns of gold, rings of stones, eyes of fire, world aflame with our beauty.

And if God makes us one, we shall be one indeed.

When one and one come together two is made and at heart is the lamb, our crown and glory.

At long last, my name is no longer a hum in your ear and neither is yours in mine.

And if God makes us one, we shall be one indeed.

When one and one come together two is made and at heart is the lamb, our crown and glory.

Betwixt us shall the little seraphims dance when we have met.

And if God makes us one, we shall be one indeed.

When one and one come together two is made and at heart is the lamb, our crown and glory.

I said go, but God said no and now I say nay and he says yea.

And if God makes us one, we shall be one indeed.

When one and one come together two is made and at heart is the lamb, our crown and glory.

Circles around my body, my heart flying away from me like a butterfly in spring.

And if God makes us one, we shall be one indeed.

When one and one come together two is made and at heart is the lamb, our crown and glory.

They shall bring vines of grapes with their cups overflowing with the Holy Spirit.

And if God makes us one, we shall be one indeed.

When one and one come together two is made and at heart is the lamb, our crown and glory.

We shall dance like young fawns with the sun gleaming down upon us so that we look like a mirror together.

And if God makes us one, we shall be one indeed.

When one and one come together two is made and at heart is the lamb, our crown and glory.

# Slipped Away in Adrift

# Out There

---

Somewhere in the clouds, your angel soul
watches me, wondering when.
I know you're out there somewhere and that in
time we will find each other.
Both of our hearts cry for another's and though at
times it seems like you're a myth, I know you can't be, for
in my heart I have an image of you that marks my heart.
I know you're out there somewhere and that in
time we will find each other.
We will one day dance endlessly together through century
after century as we had done before.
I know you're out there somewhere and that in
time we will find each other.
I know you will just come down like lightning from the
sky at night and there you are.
I know you're out there somewhere and that in
time we will find each other.

It's a tough pill to swallow to just wait while watching everyone else with someone getting off the train for them and yet I still sit on the bench and wait.

I know you're out there somewhere and that in time we will find each other.

For years my heart has cried out to God to reunite us. Only now do I realize what it cried for.

I know you're out there somewhere and that in time we will find each other.

Water dripping on my head from the skies tears and tears from my own eyes join the dew of morning.

I know you're out there somewhere and that in time we will find each other.

You won't give up, you won't step back, you won't quit, and you won't be afraid but persistent.

I know you're out there somewhere and that in time we will find each other.

Only love is persistent through anything and fake love is irresolute, no matter how true it seems, it is only one way.

I know you're out there somewhere and that in time we will find each other.

Our souls are one and so are our lives.

Don't cry. Don't fret, my love, the best is yet to come.

And we will find one another as we did in eternity.

Though we fall through this abyss to a destination unknown.

Don't cry. Don't fret, my love, the best is yet to come.

And we will find one another as we did in eternity.

Stars are our eyes, flares are our wings to fly away with.

Don't cry. Don't fret, my love, the best is yet to come.

And we will find one another as we did in eternity.

Forget not I and I forget not you so we may recognize something.

Don't cry. Don't fret, my love, the best is yet to come.

And we will find one another as we did in eternity.

Babes were we when we entered time and no one knows why we cry.

Don't cry. Don't fret, my love, the best is yet to come.

And we will find one another as we did in eternity.

I lost a part of me when I came here and I cried because when I was born part of me died and I was left behind.

Don't cry. Don't fret, my love, the best is yet to come.

And we will find one another as we did in eternity.

Kindred spirits aren't just fairy tales, they are what makes you and I whole again.

Don't cry. Don't fret, my love, the best is yet to come.

And we will find one another as we did in eternity.

Once I find you I shall swim to you through the galaxy and you shall swim to me.

Don't cry. Don't fret, my love, the best is yet to come.

And we will find one another as we did in eternity.

I will no longer cry for you embracing me is all I need to make me satisfied and happy.

Don't cry. Don't fret, my love, the best is yet to come.

And we will find one another as we did in eternity.

Finding you is finding Elysium and my home, a place I can always come back to.

Don't cry. Don't fret, my love, the best is yet to come.

And we will find one another as we did in eternity.

Family, friends, and people can come close to what I have with you.

Don’t cry. Don’t fret, my love, the best is yet to come.

And we will find one another as we did in eternity.

It's like I’ve chased you forever and then once I catch up, I’ve finally caught up to the place this entire thing stopped.

Don’t cry. Don’t fret, my love, the best is yet to come.

And we will find one another as we did in eternity.

# But If We Just Believed

---

To know that you and I are one of a kind and can't be made different or apart.

But if we just believed enough we could have what we had in eternity again and again.

And the music would be non-stop and your smile would be a light.

To know that mother and father will be always there to hold and teach you.

But if we just believed enough we could have what we had in eternity again and again.

And the music would be non-stop and your smile would be a light.

To know that one plus one is two and two plus Christ make beauty.

But if we just believed enough we could have what we had in eternity again and again.

And the music would be non-stop and your smile would be a light.

To know that I can walk, but I can't, but can if I were to know what that can was for.

But if we just believed enough we could have what we had in eternity again and again.

And the music would be non-stop and your smile would be a light.

To know that age doesn't teach and neither do years, but God does.

But if we just believed enough we could have what we had in eternity again and again.

And the music would be non-stop and your smile would be a light.

To know that being first place isn't with a medal always, not even a cheer.

But if we just believed enough we could have what we had in eternity again and again.

And the music would be non-stop and your smile would be a light.

To know that what I want isn't what I want, but is what I have already taken.

But if we just believed enough we could have what we had in eternity again and again.

And the music would be non-stop and your smile would be a light.

To know that those alike aren't alike and those that aren't alike are alike.

But if we just believed enough we could have what we had in eternity again and again.

And the music would be non-stop and your smile would be a light.

To know that taking a breath here and pausing there is fine for the mind.

But if we just believed enough we could have what we had in eternity again and again.

And the music would be non-stop and your smile would be a light.

To know that there is no real man that can predict what and who I am and where I will go.

But if we just believed enough we could have what we had in eternity again and again.

And the music would be non-stop and your smile would be a light.

To know that love is real. Agape and Eos create balance. For what is greatness without a heart and what is a heart without greatness.

# To Say On and On

---

When our life seems to be diminished
and our eyes dreary.

It is easy to say go on and on and yet
you're not the one living it.

We will get there and we will be the ones on top
even though now we die.

It is easy to say go on and on and yet
you're not the one living it.

Keep seeking, keep fighting for what
you dream of at night.

It is easy to say go on and on and yet
you're not the one living it.

When you arrive at greatness you will be
happy you didn't quit in the beginning.

It is easy to say go on and on and yet you're not the one living it.

Everyone is cheering and rooting for you the underdog all the time.

It is easy to say go on and on and yet you're not the one living it.

Continue to search and you will find what you've been looking for.

It is easy to say go on and on and yet you're not the one living it.

What you have coming is better than what you left in your past.

It is easy to say go on and on and yet you're not the one living it.

# *Wingless Angel*

---

It's all dead to me, even myself as a person.

I want to cry, I want to fly, I want to die.

Because when you left, you took with you half of me.

It's lonely because I've never had any safe haven, only home.

I want to cry, I want to fly, I want to die.

Because when you left, you took with you half of me.

It's not right, I can't continue without the other half of my heart.

I want to cry, I want to fly, I want to die.

Because when you left, you took with you half of me.

I breathe and it hurts, I cry and the only thing that comes from it is silence.

I want to cry, I want to fly, I want to die.

Because when you left, you took with you half of me.

It does me no good to look to the skies for I am stricken with blindness.

I want to cry, I want to fly, I want to die.

Because when you left, you took with you half of me.

It's like my evil days have already come upon me as the heavens have fallen.

I want to cry, I want to fly, I want to die.

Because when you left, you took with you half of me.

I reach my hand out to touch Thy face, but only grasp the air and my hope soon departeth.

I want to cry, I want to fly, I want to die.

Because when you left, you took with you half of me.

I know You have to understand, but it's like You've turned a deaf ear to my heart.

I want to cry, I want to fly, I want to die.

Because when you left, you took with you half of me.

No one understands and tells me to instantly change my perspective, but it's all in my heart, all in my chest, and wants to explode with such sadness I would die if it ever emerged.

I want to cry, I want to fly, I want to die.

Because when you left, you took with you half of me.

How can I change my perspective if I'm dead, bones can't walk when there is no soul.

I want to cry, I want to fly, I want to die.

Because when you left, you took with you half of me.

I have no spirit, no will at all to look forward to. There is no future.

I want to cry, I want to fly, I want to die.

Because when you left, you took with you half of me.

What is a future, if there is no sustenance to the past?

I want to cry, I want to fly, I want to die.

Because when you left, you took with you half of me.

Money, jewels, fame, all those things of the world I could have easily, but they will never fill the hole.

I want to cry, I want to fly, I want to die.

Because when you left, you took with you half of me.

I'm empty oh God. I'm empty and I can no longer bear to keep going on empty like this.

I want to cry, I want to fly, I want to die.

Because when you left, you took with you half of me.

I need the wings of my angel to round about me and to bring the person that is trapped inside out and help my wings that were cut off, return, otherwise I will remain here as a wingless angel.

I want to cry, I want to fly, I want to die.

Because when you left, you took with you half of me.

I can't become my true self with a snap of the fingers, if that were the case everyone could snap their fingers and I would be this person waltzing around like a clown.

I want to cry, I want to fly, I want to die.

Because when you left, you took with you half of me.

If I cannot find that one to help me find my wings, then I will not be able to fly with the other angels, and the world will know of my true self and seek my soul.

I want to cry, I want to fly, I want to die.

Because when you left, you took with you half of me.

# Before This

The length of time couldn't be measured as the hair upon our heads.

Before this, we were together and of one soul.

And then the ground quaked and we were separated by the great fault that left us reaching for one another's hand, but the gap is even further than the strength of our bond.

There wasn't such a thing as a past, present, or future we were just here in existence.

Before this, we were together and of one soul.

And then we fell, slipped off the edge like all those before us into an endless sea.

There wasn't such a thing as lost and found or even a two-way path.

Before this, we were together and of one soul.

And then the sky opened and swallowed the world as we knew it with its mouth for it wept that it couldn't have what the children below had.

There wasn't such a thing as being afraid of you or your thoughts.

Before this, we were together and of one soul.

And then the tails of that serpent wrapped around you and dragged you away from my grasp.

There wasn't such a thing as loneliness or depression because I had you then.

Before this, we were together and of one soul.

And then like a flash of lightning we were both struck with tears at birth and no one knows why except for us, for in those first few moments we remember what we lost and what is to come.

There wasn't such a thing as words to tell what was on your mind for we were one.

Before this, we were together and of one soul.

And then when we reached this Earth our souls visited that graveyard where we buried the one we lost in eternity.

# Who Needs You?

---

To tell me I'm wrong, mixed up, confused,
and all over the place.
How would you know? I mean, how could you?
You're just as dead as me.
Who needs you?
To tell me what's good for you is good for me.
Fix your mind and fix yourself.
Who needs you?
Leave me to die, then want to love me all
over again like a menace.
Get away, go away and this time don't come back.
Who needs you?

To make me feel like a person when I know I am a person.

You aren't even real, so you don't even know what a person is.

Who needs you?

Say we're friends like that's some kind of game, that's a heart you're messing with!

It's one thing to play around with dolls, but it's another with people.

Who needs you?

Families put on smiles at dinner but no one wants to be bothered with anyone, it's just what they call tolerated for the time being.

Liars and more liars and what you end up with is pain to the innocent.

Who needs you?

To be the one I look to for help or the one everyone looks up to.

If you want that much attention, then you're not setting out to really help.

# And Even with Beauty

---

I am alone without a partner by my side.

And you'd think that with beauty and all I would
be the happiest person on Earth.

But that is not so in this tale.

I don't have friends to hang out with.

And you'd think that with beauty and all I would
be the happiest person on Earth.

But that is not so in this tale.

I have a different soul and a different
Father not like the other children.

And you'd think that with beauty and all I would
be the happiest person on Earth.

But that is not so in this tale.

I shed countless tears, enough to fill the basin in
heaven that allows rain on Earth.
And you'd think that with beauty and all I would
be the happiest person on Earth.

But that is not so in this tale.

I want someone to love, but I can't find one
because they say my request is too great.
And you'd think that with beauty and all I would
be the happiest person on Earth.

But that is not so in this tale.

I want someone to pursue and fight dragons,
who won't back down and not just anyone by my
side, a prince.
And you'd think that with beauty and all I would
be the happiest person on Earth.

But that is not so in this tale.

I'm this person that has a heart without
chords to be played.
And you'd think that with beauty and all I would
be the happiest person on Earth.

But that is not so in this tale.

I don't want to be this person walking the streets, watching the world go by.
And you'd think that with beauty and all I would be the happiest person on Earth.

But that is not so in this tale.

I can't tolerate weakness, the courage to calm my high spirits is what I need.
And you'd think that with beauty and all I would be the happiest person on Earth.

But that is not so in this tale.

I change in my head, although in my heart is another song that goes on and on, the one that was written by the other half of my heart long ago.
And you'd think that with beauty and all I would be the happiest person on Earth.

But that is not so in this tale.

I will continue to search and yet the same concluding story happens with every try.
And you'd think that with beauty and all I would be the happiest person on Earth.

But that is not so in this tale.

I wonder if there is one for me or is this dream in my heart is just a mirage that is not true.
And you'd think that with beauty and all I would be the happiest person on Earth.

But that is not so in this tale.

I fall down like a broken child in frustration because all of them come at me and none of them fit the script.
And you'd think that with beauty and all I would be the happiest person on Earth.

But that is not so in this tale.

I wish to rewrite the script so that I can just accept one and go my way and hope for happiness, but I can't.
And you'd think that with beauty and all I would be the happiest person on Earth.

But that is not so in this tale.

I watch the others dance happily ever after and wonder why can't I have it just that easy.
And you'd think that with beauty and all I would be the happiest person on Earth.

But that is not so in this tale.

I have to wait, have to listen and it seems like I'm screwing it all up because opportunities are always knocking at my door and I turn every one of them down.

And you'd think that with beauty and all I would be the happiest person on Earth.

But that is not so in this tale.

In the end the curse of having beauty, not prettiness, not magnificence, but beauty is that it requires a pure heart so that it can radiate. It requires time and it requires a certain code that not just anyone can unlock, no matter how close they are, it has to be authentic like the beauty we hold.

# Viens Petit Ange

---

What is the difference between a white flower and red flower?
When your heart does tire and your heart does wire
and your eyes only desire is death.
Viens petit ange brisé for there is a way to fly again.
What is the difference between receiving and taking gifts that you do not long for?
When your heart does tire and your heart does wire
and your eyes only desire is death.
Viens petit ange brisé for there is a way to fly again.

What are the difference between a fish without water and a human without oxygen when both shall drown in the evils they couldn't see?

When your heart does tire and your heart does wire
and your eyes only desire is death.

Viens petit ange brisé for there is a way to fly again.

What is a hero without a shield and sword to fend that dragon with its fiery breath?

When your heart does tire and your heart does wire
and your eyes only desire is death.

Viens petit ange brisé for there is a way to fly again.

What is there to look for in the skies, when only fog and dirt blanket it?

When your heart does tire and your heart does wire
and your eyes only desire is death.

Viens petit ange brisé for there is a way to fly again.

What does it matter to do right when no one's there ever to help you up, even after the times you helped them?

When your heart does tire and your heart does wire
and your eyes only desire is death.

Viens petit ange brisé for there is a way to fly again.

Arrows strike my head with heaps of juniper
and stings of scorpions in my head.
When your heart does tire and your heart does wire
and your eyes only desire is death.
Viens petit ange brisé for there is a way to fly again.

Why does it matter to keep staggering through
this burning house, when there may be no way out
anyway?
When your heart does tire and your heart does wire
and your eyes only desire is death.
Viens petit ange brisé for there is a way to fly again.

Where does the sanity of our minds go as we
enter this field of the war we were drafted into?
When your heart does tire and your heart does wire
and your eyes only desire is death.
Viens petit ange brisé for there is a way to fly again.

For one moment I thought I could see the end,
but as always in the hazy battlefield dreams often trick
you into being a real destination.
When your heart does tire and your heart does wire
and your eyes only desire is death.
Viens petit ange brisé for there is a way to fly again.

Home is what the heart cries for, but we're home and home is even ablaze in flames so where is home?

When your heart does tire and your heart does wire and your eyes only desire is death.

Viens petit ange brisé for there is a way to fly again.

I thought God armed me with enough for the next battle, I never thought He was going to load it on me like this.

When your heart does tire and your heart does wire and your eyes only desire is death.

Viens petit ange brisé for there is a way to fly again.

I know He says He won't put more on me than I can bear, but God I'm dying, I'm dying and I cannot take anymore.

When your heart does tire and your heart does wire and your eyes only desire is death.

Viens petit ange brisé for there is a way to fly again.

I've been shot in the right leg, glazed on the left side of my head, and my back is pierced with arrows and God wants me to still get up and fight to get home?

When your heart does tire and your heart does wire
and your eyes only desire is death.
Viens petit ange brisé for there is a way to fly again.
Where do the bodies that thunder across the
ground go after this war of angels and man?
When your heart does tire and your heart does wire
and your eyes only desire is death.
Viens petit ange brisé for there is a way to fly again.

# Petit Rose

---

Lying here beneath an endless galaxy of possibilities.

Hush. Hush, petit rose, for thy beloved is not just a dream caught in the stars.

Crying with shame as you have broken my heart like glass once again.

Hush. Hush, petit rose, for thy beloved is not just a dream caught in the stars.

Running in circles so many voices I cannot remember yours.

Hush. Hush, petit rose, for thy beloved is not just a dream caught in the stars.

The message is within thy eyes as it is in mine, but when you act your actions speak as death.

Hush. Hush, petit rose, for thy beloved is not just a dream caught in the stars.

You left me a millennium ago and now you leave me again in the talons of the sparrow.

Hush. Hush, petit rose, for thy beloved is not just a dream caught in the stars.

My heart is driven mad for I cannot understand why the notes we play together cannot be put into words, perhaps then we'd understand one another.

Hush. Hush, petit rose, for thy beloved is not just a dream caught in the stars.

It was like tag, you chased me and caught me, then I turned around and chased you, but you were too fast at the time and I couldn't catch you.

Hush. Hush, petit rose, for thy beloved is not just a dream caught in the stars.

Out of breath, out of my wits, and at this point, I know not what to say unto thee.

Hush. Hush, petit rose, for thy beloved is not just a dream caught in the stars.

I know it's true, but when I look upon thee with another, my mind is telling me another message.

Hush. Hush, petit rose, for thy beloved is not just a dream caught in the stars.

Truth is just as scary as the monster that lies in my bed every night.

Hush. Hush, petit rose, for thy beloved is not just a dream caught in the stars.

Dreams vex my soul and I cling to my pillow as if it is you in hopes to stop the storm in my mind as I sleep.

Hush. Hush, petit rose, for thy beloved is not just a dream caught in the stars.

The very thing that awakened me in that tower was you. When I heard you I suddenly awakened from a dream I thought was my life, not realizing I was dead yet.

Hush. Hush, petit rose, for thy beloved is not just a dream caught in the stars.

Will you slay the dragon and save me to only kill me with thine own sword?

Hush. Hush, petit rose, for thy beloved is not just a dream caught in the stars.

How doth thou look into my teary eyes as I knelt before you, wishing you'd remember when we were but friends and not on this uneasy ground?

Hush. Hush, petit rose, for thy beloved is not just a dream caught in the stars.

Kiss me, tell me that you are mine and I am yours, and then at the end, we both turn to just particles of sand and neither of us cannot stop each other from vanishing.

# World on Fire

# I'm Tired God

---

I shouldn't have to pick up dirt to get somewhere, I shouldn't have to fight for everything I want.

I'm tired God, tired of not having answers, tired of not having a break anywhere.

And they say they're tired, God lighten it up somewhere I'm your child but I'm not super.

How strong do you have to be to carry this, how much time does it take for a man to see sprouts?

I'm tired God, tired of not having answers, tired of not having a break anywhere.

And they say they're tired, God lighten it up somewhere I'm your child but I'm not super.

Using technology as the only thing I can speak to, losing my mind in this fortress of emptiness.

I'm tired God, tired of not having answers, tired of not having a break anywhere.

And they say they're tired, God lighten it up somewhere I'm your child but I'm not super.

Wash these days away like my shame, take this blanket away like my nightmares do something.

I'm tired God, tired of not having answers, tired of not having a break anywhere.

And they say they're tired, God lighten it up somewhere I'm your child but I'm not super.

I shouldn't have to fight to keep a job or get one, I shouldn't have to fight to stay in school or study.

I'm tired God, tired of not having answers, tired of not having a break anywhere.

And they say they're tired, God lighten it up somewhere I'm your child but I'm not super.

Just let me lose it, let me crack up so then everyone can just have a reason to say I'm nuts stop trying to help me keep it together.

I'm tired God, tired of not having answers, tired of not having a break anywhere.

And they say they're tired, God lighten it up somewhere I'm your child but I'm not super.

Everything just goes wrong whenever I want to do something, I go right it goes left, I go up, it goes down.

I'm tired God, tired of not having answers, tired of not having a break anywhere.

And they say they're tired, God lighten it up somewhere I'm your child but I'm not super.

No matter how hard I try to make it work it doesn't no more, no matter how hard I try to piece it together the pieces pop out.

I'm tired God, tired of not having answers, tired of not having a break anywhere.

And they say they're tired, God lighten it up somewhere I'm your child but I'm not super.

Try to hold on to my parents, keep them together even if it means my punishment, try to hold this family together for as long as possible so we can have a happy life.

I'm tired God, tired of not having answers, tired of not having a break anywhere.

And they say they're tired, God lighten it up somewhere I'm your child but I'm not super.

This marriage, this friendship, this relationship just isn't happening no matter what I do, they hate, she hates me, he hates me, everyone hates me more the more I try to keep everything the same as if nothing has changed.

I'm tired God, tired of not having answers, tired of not having a break anywhere.

And they say they're tired, God lighten it up somewhere I'm your child but I'm not super.

Can't drive a car, I'll crash it and guess what I do, can't have a relationship you'll never be there and guess what I'm not and it kills me that I can't make anything or anyone understand my situation.

I'm tired God, tired of not having answers, tired of not having a break anywhere.

And they say they're tired, God lighten it up somewhere I'm your child but I'm not super.

Sorry for myself, I haven't had the time for that since I'm always feeling what others feel even when I try to keep them out, patient, you wouldn't even know half my story.

I'm tired God, tired of not having answers, tired of not having a break anywhere.

And they say they're tired, God lighten it up somewhere I'm your child but I'm not super.

People judge, people, say things and guess what I don't care just stay away from me because what I'm carrying now I don't want you to have any part of since I might hurt you.

I'm tired God, tired of not having answers, tired of not having a break anywhere.

And they say they're tired, God lighten it up somewhere I'm your child but I'm not super.

This race needs to end, I'm tired of waiting, just let it happen. Haven't I been through enough to finally see the fruits of the works of my bloody hands?

Surely I've proven that I'm faithful, surely you know that I am your child now, surely you have grown tired of watching them make fun of me tripping over my shoelaces talking about what father is going to get me for Christmas and that you've prepared a table just for me.

I'm tired God, tired of not having answers, tired of not having a break anywhere.

And they say they're tired, God lighten it up somewhere I'm your child but I'm not super.

Straw after straw, can I just run out now and give up and say that this is all over so that I can close my eyes and fall asleep in the cold to wake up to the smell of fresh gingerbread and melody that I remember somewhere in my heart?

I'm tired God, tired of not having answers, tired of not having a break anywhere.

And they say they're tired, God lighten it up somewhere I'm your child but I'm not super.

Will someone say the word, will someone wave the flag and tell me my event is over?

I'm tired God, tired of not having answers, tired of not having a break anywhere.

And they say they're tired, God lighten it up somewhere I'm your child but I'm not super.

You are drowning me, Lord, killing my little soul so that it is suffocating in hot ash can't you see that and save me?

I'm tired God, tired of not having answers, tired of not having a break anywhere.

And they say they're tired, God lighten it up somewhere I'm your child but I'm not super.

They mock me so terribly that even I am shaken by their mockery, their thoughts are so loud that even I can hear them, read them in their eyes.

I'm tired God, tired of not having answers, tired of not having a break anywhere.

And they say they're tired, God lighten it up somewhere I'm your child but I'm not super.

Enough with molding me put me on the pedestal already and crown me so that the world will see that I wasn't lying about you coming for Christmas with the things you promised me and with the fellowship of others like me I so longed to have.

I'm tired God, tired of not having answers, tired of not having a break anywhere.

And they say they're tired, God lighten it up somewhere I'm your child but I'm not super.

# Does It Ever End

---

The spinning, the twirls in my mind
when everyone is gone.
When will it ever click in that you were more
than a soldier or bones to me?
Does it ever end?
Trial error, burning wounds that scar both
my heart and self.
When will it ever click in that you were more than a
soldier or bones to me?
Does it ever end?
Clocks ticking, no return, just the great abyss to
look at each lonely morning.
When will it ever click in that you were more
than a soldier or bones to me?
Does it ever end?

Swarms of pests, vigorous runnings to light that no longer shines at the end.

When will it ever click in that you were more than a soldier or bones to me?

Does it ever end?

Shattering of mirrors, falling on and on to who knows where without memory.

When will it ever click in that you were more than a soldier or bones to me?

Does it ever end?

Plunderings of power, fighting to death forgetting even why we fight when we look around and see nothing's changed.

When will it ever click in that you were more than a soldier or bones to me?

Does it ever end?

A slip on ice, catastrophic breaks on the ice till you become one with the coldness.

When will it ever click in that you were more than a soldier or bones to me?

Does it ever end?

Stand up, fall back down into a pile of bones like the others just to be buried.

When will it ever click in that you were more than a soldier or bones to me?

Does it ever end?

Paintings on you, becoming like drawings on walls from so much you never healed from.

When will it ever click in that you were more than a soldier or bones to me?

Does it ever end?

Look one way, turn the other either way you hear their screams, their cries, even your own.

When will it ever click in that you were more than a soldier or bones to me?

Does it ever end?

Home, sanctuary, if the word didn't mean returning to a warzone you long to escape.

When will it ever click in that you were more than a soldier or bones to me?

Does it ever end?

Shape it, but looking at it you wouldn't think it was what you wanted to build.

When will it ever click in that you were more than a soldier or bones to me?

Does it ever end?

What are words, meaningless vows, empty sets of notes, or piano keys without a performer?

When will it ever click in that you were more than a soldier or bones to me?

Does it ever end?

Take a step, keep dancing the same old rhythm like all the others can't even find another way.

When will it ever click in that you were more than a soldier or bones to me?

Does it ever end?

Strong, not anymore that soul was hurt too and part of us was shot down with our fellow soldier.

When will it ever click in that you were more than a soldier or bones to me?

Does it ever end?

Recognition of laughter, memorializing means nothing except another laugh to them.

When will it ever click in that you were more than a soldier or bones to me?

Does it ever end?

Our men, their men, his or her men, doesn't even matter anymore can't tell them apart from the others now, although we wished they could've tarried longer with us, perhaps it would've shielded them from those fiery arrows.

When will it ever click in that you were more than a soldier or bones to me?

Does it ever end?

# One Right

Clouds of emptiness, days of doom.

It seems that you can never make the right decision in this world.

Heart of hate, blessings of vigor.

It seems that you can never make the right decision in this world.

Can't escape regret, can't run from Hell when it's holding on your shoulder.

It seems that you can never make the right decision in this world.

Love to mine of destruction; emotions to crack my soul like marble.

It seems that you can never make the right decision in this world.

Sorrow to be kicked, borrowed to be stabbed against a wall.

It seems that you can never make the right decision in this world.

Marriage to be carried away in the slightest tempest, baggage to be scattered abroad.

It seems that you can never make the right decision in this world.

Relate doesn't bring fate, skate doesn't make eight.

It seems that you can never make the right decision in this world.

Hands of blood, palms to hand over in turn for alms.

It seems that you can never make the right decision in this world.

Doomed if you do, doomed if you don't do.

It seems that you can never make the right decision in this world.

Two-edged swords pressed against my heart, anger forced to impart.

It seems that you can never make the right decision in this world.

Dreams become a room of mirrors, tears of hopelessness like glass.

It seems that you can never make the right decision in this world.

Departure set afar so that I tarry, Archer with only his bow to stretch me further.

It seems that you can never make the right decision in this world.

Anxiety, mine own trap of state of mind, depression, a home I was only welcomed to.

It seems that you can never make the right decision in this world.

Words of shame, pedestal of fame.

It seems that you can never make the right decision in this world.

Darkness with shadows, running backward to ghostly dead meadows.

It seems that you can never make the right decision in this world.

Overtaxation, overexploitation to bring about over-exfoliation.

It seems that you can never make the right decision in this world.

Practices of drain, weights of strain.

It seems that you can never make the right decision in this world.

Media of towers, pollution of flowers.

It seems that you can never make the right decision in this world.

Blankets to cover, magnets recover.

It seems that you can never make the right decision in this world.

Sinner the pride of this world, givers the denied of this twirled.

# Why Is It

---

I pray I try to do things the right way.

But not long after my little candle is put under darkness and smothered.

Why is it that every time I seek your face, you turn it from me?

I ask, I want something more than I already have, something better.

But not long after my little candle is put under darkness and smothered.

Why is it that every time I seek your face, you turn it from me?

I swim, I struggle as the currents of water raise their hand to push me under.

But not long after my little candle is put under darkness and smothered.

Why is it that every time I seek your face, you turn it from me?

I fight, I stand up with only the will in hopes of a future to hold me up.

But not long after my little candle is put under darkness and smothered.

Why is it that every time I seek your face, you turn it from me?

I lost one, now it seems that you're taking the last thing that makes me happy, too.

But not long after my little candle is put under darkness and smothered.

Why is it that every time I seek your face, you turn it from me?

I beg I plead with all my heart for you to not turn the wheel the other way.

But not long after my little candle is put under darkness and smothered.

Why is it that every time I seek your face, you turn it from me?

I wind, I spin like a carousel without control and now I can't see clearly.

But not long after my little candle is put under darkness and smothered.

Why is it that every time I seek your face, you turn it from me?

I kill, I slay and yet the dragon is always standing amid the door.

But not long after my little candle is put under darkness and smothered.

Why is it that every time I seek your face, you turn it from me?

# You Have Forever

I need to have someone in my life and I don't mean another twenty years later.

You have forever God, but as for me I only have a day, a tomorrow, a week, a month, a year.

But understand I am mortal and don't have forever only a now.

I require to have some kind with my age now and I don't mean in another year.

You have forever God, but as for me I only have a day, a tomorrow, a week, a month, a year.

But understand I am mortal and don't have forever only a now.

I need my ambitions to be finished so I can move to the next step and I don't mean in another fifty-five years or decade.

You have forever God, but as for me I only have a day, a tomorrow, a week, a month, a year.

But understand I am mortal and don't have forever only a now.

I need a house less this one cave in on me and I don't mean in another seven years.

You have forever God, but as for me I only have a day, a tomorrow, a week, a month, a year.

But understand I am mortal and don't have forever only a now.

I need to have a somewhat normal life, a typical one sometimes and I don't mean in another hundred years.

You have forever God, but as for me I only have a day, a tomorrow, a week, a month, a year.

But understand I am mortal and don't have forever only a now.

I need to have something that is somewhat reliable in this fragile glass called life and I don't mean in another lifetime.

You have forever God, but as for me I only have a day, a tomorrow, a week, a month, a year.

But understand I am mortal and don't have forever only a now.

I need answers, not signs, I need to hear a voice, not a ghost whisper and I don't mean in other seventy-seven years.

You have forever God, but as for me I only have a day, a tomorrow, a week, a month, a year.

But understand I am mortal and don't have forever only a now.

I need to feel happiness, see the red blossoms of early spring and I don't mean in my old age.

You have forever God, but as for me I only have a day, a tomorrow, a week, a month, a year.

But understand I am mortal and don't have forever only a now.

# Don't Let Go, Don't Give Up the Faith

Life has fallen like glass and just continues to crack and crack on us.

Don't let go. Don't give up the faith. The best is yet to come and hell knows it.

You're winning and hell and its minions are running scared.

Snatching and taking away everything we've known and have like it was never ours.

Don't let go. Don't give up the faith. The best is yet to come and hell knows it.

You're winning and hell and its minions are running scared.

The chords are broken and so is the melody we wrote years ago.

Don’t let go. Don’t give up the faith. The best is yet to come and hell knows it.

You’re winning and hell and its minions are running scared.

Light is shining and darknesses is vanishing but it is taking some time to show.

Don’t let go. Don’t give up the faith. The best is yet to come and hell knows it.

You’re winning and hell and its minions are running scared.

They are falling with every step you take forward even though they bark like wild dogs to scare you back into your coop.

Don’t let go. Don’t give up the faith. The best is yet to come and hell knows it.

You’re winning and hell and its minions are running scared.

If you stay where you are now, that's a rebel they don’t have to worry about, because if you walk through and don’t die, others will see and do the same.

Don’t let go. Don’t give up the faith. The best is yet to come and hell knows it.

You’re winning and hell and its minions are running scared.

Their eyes are like balls of fire with fury and they look scary with their fangs.

Don't let go. Don't give up the faith. The best is yet to come and hell knows it.

You're winning and hell and its minions are running scared.

Watching what you have, they don't want it to increase so why not keep you distracted?

Don't let go. Don't give up the faith. The best is yet to come and hell knows it.

You're winning and hell and its minions are running scared.

Yes, you've lost your heart. Yes, you've lost your friends. Yes, you've lost everything, but yes, God is going to give it all back tenfold and it'll be real.

Don't let go. Don't give up the faith. The best is yet to come and hell knows it.

You're winning and hell and its minions are running scared.

Depression, after depression. Betrayal, after betrayal. You're paving this road and those mountains are coming down.

Don't let go. Don't give up the faith. The best is yet to come and hell knows it.

You're winning and hell and its minions are running scared.

It'll be you lighting a match on an apple on their head and biting the top.

Don't let go. Don't give up the faith. The best is yet to come and hell knows it.

You're winning and hell and its minions are running scared.

They don't hate us, they hate that we have freedom to lead and will to fight through a beating.

Don't let go. Don't give up the faith. The best is yet to come and hell knows it.

You're winning and hell and its minions are running scared.

If they get us to shut up the rebellion stops, that's why they have to break us when we are young, otherwise, there's nothing you can do when we are old and set.

# Throwing Everything

---

I haven't got sight, but God knows I've got faith through him.

And I'm throwing everything I've got at you because I am winning this fight.

And you're going to see the champion out of the beat-up mess I am.

I know I'm on my knees now, but if I'm too weak to fight you standing I'm going to fight you below.

And I'm throwing everything I've got at you because I am winning this fight.

And you're going to see the champion out of the beat-up mess I am.

I don't know anything at this point, but I have hope that is like a flame of fire.

And I'm throwing everything I've got at you because I am winning this fight.

And you're going to see the champion out of the beat-up mess I am.

Keep putting me down, I'm still going to fight though I'm crying and angry.

And I'm throwing everything I've got at you because I am winning this fight.

And you're going to see the champion out of the beat-up mess I am.

I don't have a clue how, but I know I want to be free of this ring.

And I'm throwing everything I've got at you because I am winning this fight.

And you're going to see the champion out of the beat-up mess I am.

I don't have gloves, so I'm giving you my bare hands.

And I'm throwing everything I've got at you because I am winning this fight.

And you're going to see the champion out of the beat-up mess I am.

I don't have courage, but I do have love to push me at my opponent, for the ones I love to go further I have to beat them.

And I'm throwing everything I've got at you because I am winning this fight.

And you're going to see the champion out of the beat-up mess I am.

# I Believe

That nothing is impossible with God on your side.

I believe in the will and God's plan.

And though I do I can't shake the fear that after this one I will be crippled to my knees if this goes wrong.

I'm scared to death, trembling with every moment that I know what I have to do.

I believe in the will and God's plan.

And though I do I can't shake the fear that after this one I will be crippled to my knees if this goes wrong.

My mind is spinning and I want to run away to a faraway land to escape the task that lies in weight for me when I go back.

I believe in the will and God's plan.

And though I do I can't shake the fear that after this one I will be crippled to my knees if this goes wrong.

Though others are able to fly away from the coop in which the scorpion is in, I am cornered in the fence awaiting my death by the sting of its barb.

I believe in the will and God's plan.

And though I do I can't shake the fear that after this one I will be crippled to my knees if this goes wrong.

It is no joke, nothing to play with destiny is going to come to your door knocking whether you decide to run or fight for your destiny to take your place.

I believe in the will and God's plan.

And though I do I can’t shake the fear that after this one I will be crippled to my knees if this goes wrong.

There is no conciliation in time that goes by like the pebbles in the river.

I believe in the will and God’s plan.

And though I do I can’t shake the fear that after this one I will be crippled to my knees if this goes wrong.

This time if I fail again, it’ll come back and it’ll come back harder and harder every time until I decide to do differently.

I believe in the will and God’s plan.

And though I do I can’t shake the fear that after this one I will be crippled to my knees if this goes wrong.

It didn’t work for me ten years ago, what makes me think it’s going to work for me in another decade or so?

I believe in the will and God’s plan.

And though I do I can't shake the fear that after this one I will be crippled to my knees if this goes wrong.

I need guidance for at this point mine eyes are drowning with tears as I walk this path of delusions and vagueness.

I believe in the will and God's plan.

And though I do I can't shake the fear that after this one I will be crippled to my knees if this goes wrong.

If the thorns weren't for the flowers, to begin with, what makes you think they'll be for you when you speak of beauty?

I believe in the will and God's plan.

And though I do I can't shake the fear that after this one I will be crippled to my knees if this goes wrong.

Destroyed is my estate at this point and there seems to be no way to return home to the world I previously knew.

I believe in the will and God's plan.

And though I do I can't shake the fear that after this one I will be crippled to my knees if this goes wrong.

It doesn't matter to the comets the time it took for you to create the garden, their course is to destroy and destroy with flames.

# *And If You're Not...*

---

On the same level as us, doing the same things as us.

Then get lost. Don't come back. Go find this dream you say you believe in.

Because we don't need you to convict us of our crimes.

And if you're not…

On the same assembly line or one at all, doing what we all do.

Then get lost. Don't come back. Go find this dream you say you believe in.

Because we don't need you to convict us of our crimes.

And if you're not…

On the same ship to heaven on Earth and hell after, doing whatever we feel.

Then get lost. Don't come back. Go find this dream you say you believe in.

Because we don't need you to convict us of our crimes.

And if you're not…

On the same plane of creation, doing the dirtiest of dirt to get by.

Then get lost. Don't come back. Go find this dream you say you believe in.

Because we don't need you to convict us of our crimes.

And if you're not…

For any of the abominations in which God abhors, then you mine well accept the fact you are hated and are prey.

# And If Yeshua Loves You

---

They crown us with hate and treat us like dirt.

It takes a lot. A lot of tears and sadness to be separated like that.

But if Yeshua loves you, God knows where you will soar.

They cut our wings that we come into this world with so that our glory is dimmed.

It takes a lot. A lot of tears and sadness to be separated like that.

But if Yeshua loves you, God knows where you will soar.

They don't care for us no matter what we do for them.

It takes a lot. A lot of tears and sadness to be separated like that.

But if Yeshua loves you, God knows where you will soar.

Can't have friends, for you'll end up with a knife to the heart every time.

It takes a lot. A lot of tears and sadness to be separated like that.

But if Yeshua loves you, God knows where you will soar.

They don't love us like in the movies that make it look easy.

It takes a lot. A lot of tears and sadness to be separated like that.

But if Yeshua loves you, God knows where you will soar.

We're left to the ally by family to starve and die or to break us.

It takes a lot. A lot of tears and sadness to be separated like that.

But if Yeshua loves you, God knows where you will soar.

No one stands up for us like in the stories at times we're abandoned.

It takes a lot. A lot of tears and sadness to be separated like that.

But if Yeshua loves you, God knows where you will soar.

We've all been there looking for mother and father to pull us out of our mess and they can't anymore.

It takes a lot. A lot of tears and sadness to be separated like that.

But if Yeshua loves you, God knows where you will soar.

Looking for those people we thought we knew all those years that are now shaded.

It takes a lot. A lot of tears and sadness to be separated like that.

But if Yeshua loves you, God knows where you will soar.

With his hands that were pierced, he stretches one out to you, his garments flowing like rays of white light.

It takes a lot. A lot of tears and sadness to be separated like that.

But if Yeshua loves you, God knows where you will soar.

When we've been forgotten, forsaken, for all we were then is passed by and the world is new.

It takes a lot. A lot of tears and sadness to be separated like that.

But if Yeshua loves you, God knows where you will soar.

# It's Never Just That Simple

---

To love one at first sight, but be struck with a curse without words.

It's never just that simple to have, to be, because once my mind and heart get into it my soul no longer knows what it wants.

My mind brings up verses to convince me I'm wrong, my heart telling me to just feel and not think for a moment.

To have fame after working hard for so long, but beaten with a rod that says be humble.

It's never just that simple to have, to be, because once my mind and heart get into it my soul no longer knows what it wants.

My mind brings up verses to convince me I'm wrong, my heart telling me to just feel and not think for a moment.

To want something that you solely deserve, but troubled with thoughts that you're not the one.

It's never just that simple to have, to be, because once my mind and heart get into it my soul no longer knows what it wants.

My mind brings up verses to convince me I'm wrong, my heart telling me to just feel and not think for a moment.

To waltz from one side of the room beautifully and yet have a slipper untied.

It's never just that simple to have, to be, because once my mind and heart get into it my soul no longer knows what it wants.

My mind brings up verses to convince me I'm wrong, my heart telling me to just feel and not think for a moment.

# There is Only Me

---

To protect myself from the fiery arrows that seek my heart.

There is only me.

Not a somebody, not a someone, or a something.

To understand what I feel in certain moments of time that pause like mirrors.

There is only me.

Not a somebody, not a someone, or a something.

To understand what I mean when I put words into voice around others.

There is only me.

Not a somebody, not a someone, or a something.

To understand what it is, my heart truly aches and cries to have.

There is only me.

Not a somebody, not a someone, or a something.

To understand what it feels like to have your child of sparkling eyes ripped from your arms.

There is only me.

Not a somebody, not a someone, or a something.

To understand why I cannot be stable in happiness even when I have more.

There is only me.

Not a somebody, not a someone, or a something.

To understand what it means to die day after day in that same place you died long ago.

There is only me.

Not a somebody, not a someone, or a something.

To understand what it means to feel the hurt of loss and being burned in hellfire.

There is only me.

Not a somebody, not a someone, or a something.

To understand what it means to be this person in a dark area in a small circle of light putting you on the spot.

There is only me.

Not a somebody, not a someone, or a something.

To understand what turned me to be this cold toward everyone in this world.

There is only me.

Not a somebody, not a someone, or a something.

To understand why I made and make bad decisions continually that harms me and others.

There is only me.

Not a somebody, not a someone, or a something.

To understand why I don't care, don't love, don't feel just standing here as an empty corpse of a living dead person. Because what is a house without inhabitants to light the candles and give that place its name called home?

# In the Shadows

# Asunder

---

Sparks. Light. Shadows. Beings and from the depths they rise like traces of ash.

With his grappling hold of thunder, he takes us all asunder.

It's like the world is turned upside down and you're hanging like a bat from the ground.

With his grappling hold of thunder, he takes us all asunder.

Words proceed from tongues like vipers, biting vindictively at prey bringing tears to their eyes.

With his grappling hold of thunder, he takes us all asunder.

Might. Courage. Not even close to keeping you from performing the waltz he has created for us all to dance.

With his grappling hold of thunder, he takes us all asunder.

Feet tap and clatter as if they have a mind of their own; for it is the price we pay for our choices.

With his grappling hold of thunder, he takes us all asunder.

Burning like hot embers of the fireplace as one by one the pieces pile into ash.

With his grappling hold of thunder, he takes us all asunder.

Look one way, turn the other as our master continues to keep us in this ring we long to end.

With his grappling hold of thunder, he takes us all asunder.

It is a perpetual story we all wanted to read and venture into that chapter we longed to see.

With his grappling hold of thunder, he takes us all asunder.

Deaf ears could even hear the tapping of shoes, the screaming of voices, and the roaring of the tempest.

With his grappling hold of thunder, he takes us all asunder.

Sitting on the chair crowned with glory that slowly became shame as we couldn't help but start the waltz.

With his grappling hold of thunder, he takes us all asunder.

Circles coil to more circles when you think one has ended and you are forced to continue waltzing by.

With his grappling hold of thunder, he takes us all asunder.

Hours, day, time, all turn into eternity as you wonder when the waltz will be over.

With his grappling hold of thunder, he takes us all asunder.

Changing faces, voices, even the image you pictured everything that should've been are all being mimicked by that shadow you so longed to waltz with.

With his grappling hold of thunder, he takes us all asunder.

Weary, can't even believe what has happened which is like something from the unreal.

With his grappling hold of thunder, he takes us all asunder.

On the count of five, the planks of the floor grow narrower until it completely breaks from the weight.

With his grappling hold of thunder, he takes us all asunder.

Words like fiery arrows devour everything with all misinterpretations and little thought.

With his grappling hold of thunder, he takes us all asunder.

One by one the others in the waltz start to fall like dominoes all around you.

With his grappling hold of thunder, he takes us all asunder.

# Tomorrow

---

It came knocking on my front door like a tax collector.

And there I was standing, waiting for the next day but when tomorrow came I was standing in it unprepared.

Wasted time came and devoured my youth and left me frail and nothing.

And there I was standing, waiting for the next day but when tomorrow came I was standing in it unprepared.

The glow of innocence in mine eyes is replaced by the echoes of the ghost that haunts me until death does its part.

And there I was standing, waiting for the next day but when tomorrow came I was standing in it unprepared.

Love came and love went away for I was afraid to try and step out on faith and the only thing that loved me was my money.

And there I was standing, waiting for the next day but when tomorrow came I was standing in it unprepared.

One, two, three my body begins to betray me like all those that you thought would stay in your life forever.

And there I was standing, waiting for the next day but when tomorrow came I was standing in it unprepared.

Wrinkle my clock in hopes that I can stop it, but what good are reins of a mule without a master?

And there I was standing, waiting for the next day but when tomorrow came I was standing in it unprepared.

Protruding from my lungs are those evils I did in my youth that I cursed myself with.

And there I was standing, waiting for the next day but when tomorrow came I was standing in it unprepared.

Surely I headed for the door to get upon that train but I had forgotten my ticket to where I was supposed to go.

And there I was standing, waiting for the next day but when tomorrow came I was standing in it unprepared.

When the gate to tomorrow opened, the sad part was when he came I wasn't packed and ready to go meet him and so like all conductors, he had to leave me behind to take on the passengers that had been ready for the next ride and now I ride any train of tomorrow that will accept me and till this day I remain lost wishing I had been ready for the arrival of tomorrow the first time.

# If We Don't Fly Now

Left to die of famine in the dead of winter.

If we don't fly now we will perish in the winter's storm.

So many memories in this place that only live in these walls.

If we don't fly now we will perish in the winter's storm.

The thought of starving, both in the Winter and the loss of what you had then will eat you alive.

If we don't fly now we will perish in the winter's storm.

Grasping hold of your fragile white wings and breaking them, although they were almost already broken.

If we don't fly now we will perish in the winter's storm.

It's chilling breath breathing in your face and sending you swirling throughout the air as if you are caught in a whirlpool in the air.

If we don't fly now we will perish in the winter's storm.

There are two things that stop a bird from flying in the Winter, being too weak or just too afraid to leave behind what it has or had.

If we don't fly now we will perish in the winter's storm.

They say there is more in the Summerland, but you don't care to have more, you only care to have what you had.

If we don't fly now we will perish in the winter's storm.

At first Winter with his famine will be as beautiful as gems, only to freeze you and make you believe you're still alive without realizing it's just the effects of Winter frost before death.

If we don't fly now we will perish in the winter's storm.

Hate for Summer stems from the ugly truth of facing the sun, love for Winter is because of the elusiveness of the snow.

If we don't fly now we will perish in the winter's storm.

Steady and slowly you can't help approach the stone covered in snow that you're convinced is the living memory of your past.

If we don't fly now we will perish in the winter's storm.

# Leaving Behind the Known

Because at least here I know how to try and escape hell.

Leaving behind the known for the unknown is scarier than walking off a cliff.

To know what I'm in is bad, but what is over there I might not make it.

Because at least here I can outrun the demons for a while as they chase me.

Leaving behind the known for the unknown is scarier than walking off a cliff.

To know what I'm in is bad, but what is over there I might not make it.

Because at least here I can lie to myself that I am still in the past when it was good.

Leaving behind the known for the unknown is scarier than walking off a cliff.

To know what I'm in is bad, but what is over there I might not make it.

Because if I just so much as open the door to another route I could die.

Leaving behind the known for the unknown is scarier than walking off a cliff.

To know what I'm in is bad, but what is over there I might not make it.

Because if I so much as think of freedom, think of a better life I might break.

Leaving behind the known for the unknown is scarier than walking off a cliff.

To know what I'm in is bad, but what is over there I might not make it.

Because walking in darkness I don't have to see the fear, but if there is light I will see it all and be brought back to tears.

Leaving behind the known for the unknown is scarier than walking off a cliff.

To know what I'm in is bad, but what is over there I might not make it.

Because falling daily means the more scars I will get and they won't heal but worsen.

Leaving behind the known for the unknown is scarier than walking off a cliff.

To know what I'm in is bad, but what is over there I might not make it.

Because taking God's hand is scary if there is no answer, so staying safe means staying dead unto death.

Leaving behind the known for the unknown is scarier than walking off a cliff.

To know what I'm in is bad, but what is over there I might not make it.

Because being numb means having no kind of feeling, just the thought of being here.

Leaving behind the known for the unknown is scarier than walking off a cliff.

To know what I'm in is bad, but what is over there I might not make it.

Because everyone is out here to just survive the moment, who cares to take it a step further.

Leaving behind the known for the unknown is scarier than walking off a cliff.

To know what I'm in is bad, but what is over there I might not make it.

Because dying in a famine is worse than dying in a land with plenty of poisoned food.

Leaving behind the known for the unknown is scarier than walking off a cliff.

To know what I'm in is bad, but what is over there I might not make it.

Because the illusion in my mind is saying something totally different than what my heart knows.

Leaving behind the known for the unknown is scarier than walking off a cliff.

To know what I'm in is bad, but what is over there I might not make it.

Because it's all these realities versus reality in which now I truly don't understand.

Leaving behind the known for the unknown is scarier than walking off a cliff.

To know what I'm in is bad, but what is over there I might not make it.

Because there is this thing that told me I have so many opportunities if I stay, whereas if I go all these opportunities crumble like cities into the earth.

Leaving behind the known for the unknown is scarier than walking off a cliff.

To know what I'm in is bad, but what is over there I might not make it.

Because if taking a step further means more than just getting my daily meal, means more than me just getting sleep, and that I could lack all of these in the process, it's downright a living horror to go out there beyond the wall and suddenly wonder. What will become of me if I just as so much keep walking out here? Keep chasing after something only my heart and God knows. Leaving behind the known for the unknown is scarier than walking off a cliff. To know what I'm in is bad, but what is over there I might not make it.

# Tomorrow

---

It came knocking on my front door like a tax collector.

And there I was standing, waiting for the next day but when tomorrow came I was standing in it unprepared.

Wasted time came and devoured my youth and left me frail and nothing.

And there I was standing, waiting for the next day but when tomorrow came I was standing in it unprepared.

The glow of innocence in mine eyes is replaced by the echoes of the ghost that haunts me until death does its part.

And there I was standing, waiting for the next day but when tomorrow came I was standing in it unprepared.

Love came and love went away for I was afraid to try and step out on faith and the only thing that loved me was my money.

And there I was standing, waiting for the next day but when tomorrow came I was standing in it unprepared.

One, two, three my body begins to betray me like all those that you thought would stay in your life forever.

And there I was standing, waiting for the next day but when tomorrow came I was standing in it unprepared.

Wrinkle my clock in hopes that I can stop it, but what good are reins of a mule without a master?

And there I was standing, waiting for the next day but when tomorrow came I was standing in it unprepared.

Protruding from my lungs are those evils I did in my youth that I cursed myself with.

And there I was standing, waiting for the next day but when tomorrow came I was standing in it unprepared.

Surely I headed for the door to get upon that train but I had forgotten my ticket to where I was supposed to go.

And there I was standing, waiting for the next day but when tomorrow came I was standing in it unprepared.

When the gate to tomorrow opened, the sad part was when he came I wasn't packed and ready to go meet him and so like all conductors, he had to leave me behind to take on the passengers that had been ready for the next ride and now I ride any train of tomorrow that will accept me and till this day I remain lost wishing I had been ready for the arrival of tomorrow the first time.

# Stop Dancing for his Advocates

---

Thrust around without control of yourself for their sakes.

Enough is enough.

It's time to stop dancing for the devil's advocates and jumping when they say jump.

Engraving the mark of the beast in everyone's foreheads, but mine for me I already have a master.

Enough is enough.

It's time to stop dancing for the devil's advocates and jumping when they say jump.

They're never going to love you, for they hate the one in our hearts that shines.

Enough is enough.

It's time to stop dancing for the devil's advocates and jumping when they say jump.

# Locked Clock

# Forget Us

---

Like a bat out of the mouth of hades.
But not once did he forget us.
They came; they smote; scorned our beloved.
Tears of pure sorrow burning his face when he wept.
But not once did he forget us.
They came; they smote; scorned our beloved.
Droplets of blood that overfill his wooden cup that was given to him at the last supper.
But not once did he forget us.
They came; they smote; scorned our beloved.
The desperateness of humanity whimpering like a helpless babe.
But not once did he forget us.
They came; they smote; scorned our beloved.

The time came for the death of the church clothed in crimson raiment.

But not once did he forget us.

They came; they smote; scorned our beloved.

Giving him an iron rod for bread and a sword for a heart.

Crying out Abba Father, who turned his back on him because of our wretched state.

But not once did he forget us.

They came; they smote; scorned our beloved.

How shall we fear that he will forget us now when he came and drank up the cup?

But not once did he forget us.

They came; they smote; scorned our beloved.

Though we yet hated him, he kissed our wounds with his death and resurrection.

But not once did he forget us.

They came; they smote; scorned our beloved.

Told him he was crazy, called him the devil when he was the Messiah here to save us.

But not once did he forget us.

They came; they smote; scorned our beloved.

How can we give up when our Lord gave up so much so we could have a chance?

But not once did he forget us.

They came; they smote; scorned our beloved.

If you won't have strength for yourself, then get your strength from those that came before and remember what he went through to get you here.

But not once did he forget us.

They came; they smote; scorned our beloved.

Light on fire, he gave us a fire so we could put our gifts into the work to do what he did. Gave everything to save others and bring to them the truth.

But not once did he forget us.

They came; they smote; scorned our beloved.

We live our lives with a cross we will die on and be resurrected so that they may believe as Christ did for us, though we carry a far smaller cross than him.

But not once did he forget us.

They came; they smote; scorned our beloved.

Don't forget the weaker brethren, the needy in heart. This is why we all die so the next one can come and take the torch and run further than us before.

# And As Close As We Were

---

To honor, to love, and wealth it suddenly became too far to touch.

And as close as we were the door did yet shut before our eyes and we wept.

And I guess even through all and all God decided to turn us back to the wilderness.

Passing through the Red sea, passing through the wilderness like a sea of ants.

And as close as we were the door did yet shut before our eyes and we wept.

And I guess even through all and all God decided to turn us back to the wilderness.

Through our tears and our cries, through our sighs and complaints, we now lie dead.

And as close as we were the door did yet shut before our eyes and we wept.

And I guess even through all and all God decided to turn us back to the wilderness.

Perhaps it would be best if we hadn't departed from Egypt, departed from known land.

And as close as we were the door did yet shut before our eyes and we wept.

And I guess even through all and all God decided to turn us back to the wilderness.

Curses by day with the sun on our backs and curses by night with darkness on our eyes.

And as close as we were the door did yet shut before our eyes and we wept.

And I guess even through all and all God decided to turn us back to the wilderness.

Dies are cast and each time we are turned back to the fires of hell and the underworld.

And as close as we were the door did yet shut
before our eyes and we wept.
And I guess even through all and all God decided
to turn us back to the wilderness.
A great sea did I swim only to be
swallowed by a great fish.
And as close as we were the door did yet shut
before our eyes and we wept.
And I guess even through all and all God decided
to turn us back to the wilderness.
We dreamt the dream of the promised land and
though we couldn't get there we saw its gifts,
tasted the rivers that flowed with honey.
And as close as we were the door did yet shut
before our eyes and we wept.
And I guess even through all and all God decided
to turn us back to the wilderness.

# I Can't Say

---

Your works are evil and thy tongue is a viper that protrudes from thy mouth.

I can't say who is, I can't say who isn't saved, but for you to be this evil you cannot be human.

To strike me upon the head when it is already lowered, to stab my side when it already bleeds.

I can't say who is, I can't say who isn't saved, but for you to be this evil you cannot be human.

Killed my children with the end of a sword, smote them on the head, and burned them in hellfire like nothing.

I can't say who is, I can't say who isn't saved, but for you to be this evil you cannot be human.

Chopped the son of man like meat, devoured the souls of light like food.

I can't say who is, I can't say who isn't saved, but for you to be this evil you cannot be human.

Kick them in their foreheads since they're not marked with the sign of the beast you mark them with your foot to break their crown.

I can't say who is, I can't say who isn't saved, but for you to be this evil you cannot be human.

Put my beloved on a cross without a cause, treated him inhumanely.

I can't say who is, I can't say who isn't saved, but for you to be this evil you cannot be human.

Beat us with scorpion tails, nailed us with the tusks of elephants.

I can't say who is, I can't say who isn't saved, but for you to be this evil you cannot be human.

# In Sin

---

To grow in hopes of me taking a step further beyond her and my father.

In sin did my mother conceive me, but as a blessing from God.

Holding me tightly in her arms as she rocked me, singing to me giving me the name Zohar.

To not just lie in these evils and say I accept and I'm content with just staying that from birth.

In sin did my mother conceive me, but as a blessing from God.

Holding me tightly in her arms as she rocked me, singing to me giving me the name Zohar.

To be a light unto this world, even if those before me were dark.

In sin did my mother conceive me, but as a blessing from God.

Holding me tightly in her arms as she rocked me, singing to me giving me the name Zohar.

To be another chance to turn back what my ancestry has cursed us with and not be like them.

In sin did my mother conceive me, but as a blessing from God.

Holding me tightly in her arms as she rocked me, singing to me giving me the name Zohar.

To not be a person who uses their birth of sin as a ticket to sin in this world.

In sin did my mother conceive me, but as a blessing from God.

Holding me tightly in her arms as she rocked me, singing to me giving me the name Zohar.

To carry the wagon stage from your past generations to the hill where behold Christ stands.

In sin did my mother conceive me, but as a blessing from God.

Holding me tightly in her arms as she rocked me, singing to me giving me the name Zohar.

To come up with sorry excuses, but to use everything I have, that God has given me though I'm a sinner to change that title.

In sin did my mother conceive me, but as a blessing from God.

Holding me tightly in her arms as she rocked me, singing to me giving me the name Zohar.

To let the breath of life he has given each of us become the life we share with others in this life.

In sin did my mother conceive me, but as a blessing from God.

Holding me tightly in her arms as she rocked me, singing to me giving me the name Zohar.

To show the world that God gives chances to the ones unlikely for we the children are the hope, the gift given from God to give every being in this world even the evil a chance. A chance to have someone in their line to take the step and make the right choice somewhere along the line.